I ALWAYS TELL THE TRUTH
(EVEN IF I HAVE TO LIE TO DO IT!)

Stories from The Adirondack Liars' Club

I ALWAYS TELL THE TRUTH
(EVEN IF I HAVE TO LIE TO DO IT!)

Stories from The Adirondack Liars' Club

Edited by Vaughn Ward

Illustrations by Deborah Delaney

The Greenfield Review Press
Greenfield Center, New York

ISBN 0-912678-79-8
Library of Congress #89-82424

FIRST EDITION

Bowman Books # 4

Bowman Books is an imprint of The Greenfield Review Press. All of the volumes in this series are devoted to contemporary tellings of traditional tales.

The Greenfield Review Press
2 Middle Grove Road, P.O. Box 308
Greenfield Center, New York 12833

*This book is dedicated to
the memories of Sarah Cleveland,
Lawrence Older, and Lena Spencer.
Their spirits live on in the voices of
the new generation.*

PHOTO CREDITS

CONTENTS

Shanty at Stony Creek (*courtesy of Martha Older*)

Log Drive on Sacandaga River (*courtesy of Priscilla Edwards, Town of Edinburg Historian*)

Loggers with Peavies (*courtesy of Priscilla Edwards*)

Driving down the River (*courtesy of Priscilla Edwards*)

Early Logging Camp (*courtesy of Priscilla Edwards*)

Tennant's Mill, Town of Edinburg (*courtesy of Priscilla Edwards*)

Grampa Jesse Bowman's Store

Downtown Ballston Spa (*courtesy of Chris Morley*)

Vaughn Ward

Vaughn Ramsey Ward has been collecting, performing, and presenting the traditions of the Lower Adirondack region for twenty years. She is a graduate of the University of New Mexico, where she studied music, art history, and English, and of the Bread Loaf School of English, Middlebury College, Vermont. She studied American Folk Culture at the Cooperstown Graduate Program of the State University of New York at Oneonta. Mrs. Ward has taught English, humanities, and folklore in high school and in college. She works currently as the staff folklorist for the Lower Adirondack Regional Arts Council in Glens Falls, New York. She is married to musician, composer, and folklorist George Ward. The Wards live near the old Erie Canal in Rexford, New York, with their two teenage sons, Peter and Nathaniel, and their three cats.

INTRODUCTION

. . . History was daily being reshaped downtown, even by the quiet ones. That's one thing about tale-telling and history both: it takes two. Listening is belief . . . You cannot tickle your own self. Try it.

— Allan Gurganus, *The Oldest Living Confederate Widow Tells All*

Lies were the social stuff of the Adirondack live-in lumber camp. Today, men gather at the local diner, bar, or convenience mart to swap tall stories. And a *swap* it must be: one man offers an anecdote — understated, stretched, straight-faced. Without breaking the pace, or admitting that this is fiction, the next person carries on in the same mode. They are not, it must be said, engaging in a contest where there are winners and losers. The easy exchange of the liars' bench can be a strategy for getting around more destructive rivalry, a device for reducing yesterday's scare to today's saga of fantastic mastery. Traditional Adirondack liars are *collaborators in an ensemble effort*, participants in a community perfor-mance which links them to the first settlers in this new wild land and to the yarnspinners of the ancient world. Lying, as an art form, can flourish only within a moral system where telling the truth is taken for granted. (See Robert Bethke. *Adirondack Voices: Woodsmen and Woodslore.* Chicago: University of Chicago Press, 1981, and Barre Tolken. *The Dynamics of Folklore.* Boston: Houghton Mifflin, 1979).

The tradition of exchanging extravagant talk is very old. The first recorded tall tale motifs, the "frozen words" and a joke about a drunk who answers his spilling jug, appear in the works of Aristophanes, the Greek satirical playwright, in the third century B.C. The braggart is a stock character in the works of Plautus, a Roman comic playwright in the second century B.C. and in the miracle play cycles traditional in Medieval England. *Flyting*, a ritual contest of braggadoccio and formulaic insult, is reported in the eighth-century Anglo-Saxon epic, *Beowulf*, and, from the twentieth century, as the rhyming invective of African American youths, the *dozens*. By the eighteenth century, there were printed collections of tall tales, including most of the narratives currently in oral circulation. *Singular Travels, Campaigns, and Adventures of Baron Munchausen*, printed in Germany about 1730, was translated into English. The little book was read widely, both in England and in the colonies. The main character, Baron Munchausen, is a direct descendent of the *miles gloriosus*, the braggart soldier of earlier traditions, and an ancestor of the heroes of localized tall tales, such as the sagas about Bill Greenfield, Saratoga County's *Munchausen*. These accounts went back and forth

6

between print and oral circulation, with such notable contributors to the traditions as Benjamin Franklin, Ethan Allen, William Byrd, and John James Audubon. (Carolyn S. Brown. *The Tall Tale in American Folklore and Literature*. Knoxville: University of Tennessee Press, 1987; Walter Blair. *Horse Sense in American Humor from Benjamin Franklin to Ogden Nash*. Chicago: University of Chicago Press, 1942; Ernest W. Baughman. *Type of Motif Index of the Folktales of England and North America*. The Hague: Mouton and Co., 1966; Dorothy Dondore. "Big Talk! The Flyting, the Bage, and the Frontier Boast." *American Speech* 6, 1930, 45–55.)

The immense scale, the extremes of weather, the seriousness and danger of life in the New World seemed tall tales in themselves. The frontier, both marvelous and menacing, was perfect soil for re-planted big stories. Outrageous understatement was a kind of reverse bragging, a slow-talking bucking up in the presence of immoderate circumstances. Comedy, Aristotle suggested, purges fear and self-importance. (Constance Rourke. *American Humor: A Study in the National Character*, 1931; Mody Boatwright. *Folk Laughter on the American Frontier*. New York: Macmillan, 1949.)

Folk tales are *formulaic oral literature*, told among men who share a common work and community history. They seem to be transmitted in much the same way as Serbo-Croatian narratives, American "folk" sermons and the Homeric epics. The narratives are not memorized *ver batim*; rather, a store of motifs, fragments and anecdotes are combined, recombined, localized and embellished according to the skill of the raconteur. The art is learned by imitation and assimilation. Gifted youngsters, attracted to elders and to their yarns, spend a long time listening and taking in without joining in. They absorb, unconsciously, the structure of the tales, the pacing, and the techniques of embellishment. More deliberately, they learn the formulas they will later use in their tellings. The apprentice-tellers add to their repertoires, not by memorizing texts, but by practicing until they can compose and recompose stories. As they move into the adult tale performance group, they continue to accumulate and to recombine formulas and themes, preserving tradition as they adapt it. (Alfred B. Lord. *The Singer of Tales*. New York: Atheneum, 1971; Bruce A. Rosenberg. *The Art of the American Folk Preacher*. New York: Oxford University Press, 1970; Gerald L. Davis. *I Got the Word in Me and I Can Sing it, You Know*. Philadelphia: University of Pennsylvania, 1985.)

The best raconteurs, the ones most respected and enjoyed in their communities, usually begin their tales with factual anecdotes full of specific details. Imperceptibly, they improve on the truth, building to an explosion of crazy exaggerations: an eruption into the magical — and sometimes grotesque — illogic of ancient fairy tales. Trickster and numskull motifs become attached to stories about local characters. Often these are used to illustrate some facet of the local hero's personality. In these cases, the old stories may be "told for true," and passed on as part of local history. The tall tale braggart, the trickster, and the numskull are comic heros who survive in an unpredictable and sometimes hostile world by adapting, by luck, by being smart, and by being balanced. (For a full discussion of the comic hero and the comic rhythm, see: Wylie Syper. "The Meaning of Comedy"; Suzanne Langer. "The Comic Rhythm." Both essays are included in Robert W. Corrigan, ed. *Comedy: Meaning and Form*. Scranton, Pa.: Chandler Publishing Company, 1965.)

The wonderful talkers featured in *I Always Tell the Truth* represent the range and application of Adirondack tall tale material—factual and otherwise. This group of men met in 1985, at a party for Bill Smith and George Ward, who were performing a concert of traditional Adirondack music and stories at the Saratoga County Historical Society's Brookside Museum in Ballston Spa. Elliot Older, Bill Smith, Tim Kavanaugh, Chris Morley, and the Richards brothers spent the intermission in a session reminiscent of those gatherings in the lumbercamp social room Lawrence Older called the "Rams' Pasture." They had just met—but they all knew the routine. No one missed a beat or cracked a smile. *This* was too good to leave unnoticed on the museum porch!

The next day, Bill, Elliott, and I planned the first meeting of the Liars' Club. Everyone agreed that Larry Morrison, Harvey Carr, and Joe Bruchac belonged on the liars' bench and that walk-in liars were welcome. On October 22, 1986, the Liars' Club met to share a potluck supper and a few big ones with a large and willing audience. It was very appropriate that this first session was at the Middle Grove United Methodist Church at the foot of Lake Desolation Road. It is the home church of the Older family, a spot where woodsmen who came home for the weekend would stop Sunday night to see their neighbors on their way back into the camps in the woods around Lake Desolation.

Since that night, the Liars' Club has been featured at several upstate New York festivals and on National Public Radio. Most of their appearances have been helped along with public funds from the Folk Arts Program of the New York State Council on the Arts, whose support of traditional art forms has made a difference in the lives of so many tradition bearers. Now, thanks to the dedication and patience of Joe Bruchac of The Greenfield Review Press, the words of this generation of liars have been frozen again — this time in print.

It is an honor to have been a sort of midwife to this process. I love these talented men because they make me laugh. I love them for the savvy they share between laughs. They are wise enough not to take themselves seriously. And honest enough to tell a good, gentle lie.

Vaughn Ward
Rexford, New York
February 1990

Joe Bruchac

Joe Bruchac, born in 1942, is a lifelong resident of the Saratoga County hamlet of Greenfield Center. His father, a Slovakian, was known as "The Adirondack Taxidermist." His great-grandfather was a logger who died on a log drive on the Kennebec. His grandfather, Jesse Bowman, was an Abenaki woodsman whose influence led to Joe's interest in Native American and woods lore. Lawrence Older, one of the most important bearers of woods traditions, lived four miles away in Middle Grove. Older was a close boyhood friend of Bruchac's grandfather. (Family tradition has it that Bowman and Older, at the age of about twelve, briefly ran away to join the circus.)

The country boys and girls from Greenfield Center and Middle Grove went to high school in Saratoga Springs, where they learned to deny or conceal their woods ways — including the characteristic sense of humor. Joe's heritage from his Grandmother Bowman, a Skidmore graduate, helped him to reconcile these two worlds. Her influence led him to attend Cornell University and Syracuse University, after which he taught for three years in West Africa. He is the author of 25 books and chapbooks of his own poetry and fiction, and he is the recipient of prestigious awards and fellowships. He commands great international respect as a teller of Native American stories. With his wife, Carol, he operates *The Greenfield Review Press*. Joe Bruchac is part clever trickster, part scholar, part poet, part teacher, part woodsman. When he sits on the liars' bench, however, Joe Bruchac is Jesse Bowman's grandson and Lawrence Older's neighbor.

15

GRAMPA JESSE AND THE USED NAILS

Last July I was doing some fixing around the old house my Grandfather Jesse built. While I was taking off some of the siding I came to a layer of old wooden shingles. Shakes is what folks used to call them, handmade and split from a log. As I was prying them off I noticed something strange. Just about every one of them had extra holes in them — as if nails had been driven in and then pulled out. But then I remembered I was working on the south side of the house and I slapped my leg. That was it, all right! Grampa Jesse and those used nails.

Grampa Jesse was a man who saved things. He kept balls of twine, old newspapers, broken furniture. He saved pieces of board, old tobacco tins, cigar boxes. He didn't hold much with throwing away things that might of been old and a little bunged up but still had some use left in them, even if it was only to prop up something else that was lacking a leg or otherwise in need of repair. He wore an old beach jacket that was threadbare and had holes in its pockets from his habit of sticking his pipe into it still lit because he hated to waste the tobacco when he had smoked all he cared to. Many a time as a child I would have to tell him, "Grampa, you're on fire," and then watch him pound out a smoking pocket with his palms. I still have his old hammer. That hammer had been his grandfather's. It was in our family so long that its handle had been changed four times and the head twice. It was easy to understand why it had such sentimental value for him. That hammer saved him once from a bad fall, too. One summer evening he was up on the roof working. He was never one afraid of heights, maybe because of the Indian blood in him. That evening, though, he put his hammer down when he'd finished and stepped back onto his ladder to take a look at what he'd done. Unfortunately, the top rung of that ladder was so worn out that it broke right through and he began to fall. He was halfway down to the ground and would have broken something for sure if he hadn't remembered he'd left his hammer up on the roof and had to go back up to get it. So you can see why he prized that old hammer.

Now other folks knew that Grampa Jesse was one for saving things and so they often let him know when there was something that they were getting rid of that they figured he might be able to use. That was how he came by those shingles. It seems that Ray Ormsby, up around Lake Desolation, had a camp that was going to fix up. The first thing Ray did was to take off the old wooden shingles. He didn't just do it any which a way, like folks do now, but he pulled out all the nails and piled the shingles on the ground. Then he sent word by one of the Daniels boys that anybody who wanted those old shingles could have 'em, first come, first served. When Grampa Jesse heard about those shingles it was supper time. It was late summer and the days were still good and long, but there was no way he could have taken his team up the ten miles to Lake Desolation before it got dark. Grama Bowman tried to talk him out of it, but his mind was made up quicker than a cat can lick an ear.

"The least you can do," she said, "is wait till after supper to go, if you're so sot on climbing Fool's hill in a hurry."

Now Grampa Jesse had been working all day and he was hungry enough to eat a horse and chase its rider, so he agreed. He sat down, gulped his dinner and then went out to hitch up the team. Now when it came to horses, he always had the best. Some would be content to have a horse old enough to have been in Adam's stable, but not Grampa Jesse. His horses were generally known to be the finest team in the country, the strongest pullers and the fastest racers. Whenever he was cutting wood he'd use those horses and they gave him sort of an unfair advantage. Where other people would be just cutting down the straight trees so they could get good saw logs out of them Grampa Jesse would cut even the crooked ones, hitch that team of his on when one of those crooked logs was down and just draw it out straight. Since it

19

was dark, though, when he set out, he knew he couldn't take that team fast as they could go. They might run over some poor folks out walking on the road if they was to go at full speed. So, with lanterns lit on his rig, he set out for Lake Desolation and reached Ray Ormsby's camp just about midnight.

Now luckily for Grampa Jesse, there was a full moon that night and with the light from that moon and the lanterns on his wagon he could see just about as good as in the day time. Or at least he would have been able to if he'd been wearing glasses that had the right prescription. The glasses he had were ones that had been left him by one of his uncles. Since his own eyesight was a little weak when it came to things up close, he took along those glasses to help him out some. It made things look a little wavery, sort of like he was looking around under water, but it was clear enough that those glasses had plenty of seeing left in them and it would have been a waste not to use them. He began picking up those shingles and piling them into the wagon. It was a clear night without a cloud in the sky. As he worked it was getting colder and he could tell that come the next morning there'd be a late summer frost on the ground, the sort we get up in the mountain even in July at times. Looking around at his feet, he saw that Ray Ormsby had just dropped the old bent nails there too. He picked one of those brown nails up and he could see it was still strong enough to straighten out and use.

He always loved straightening out old nails and could bend a nail true with one quick pound faster than most people could draw a breath. So he began to picking those nails up and filling the pockets of his beach jacket with them.

When he was done gathering up the nails and the shingles, it must have been close to three in the morning. His horses had gotten a rest, sleeping as they stood there, so he just climbed up, snapped the reins and they went down that mountain so fast they were home before the sun was up. Grampa Jesse pulled right up on the lawn, which was all white with frost by now, hopped off and took a look at the south side of the house where he was planning to put those shingles. He wasn't feeling at all tired, so he decided to get right to work. He grabbed a shingle off the wagon, picked up his old hammer and reached into his pocket to get one of those bent nails he'd salvaged. That was when he discovered that pocket had a hole in it and all the nails had fallen out. He put on those old glasses and peered around and, sure enough, there all around his feet he could make out the shapes of those brown twisty old nails. So he just reached down, grabbed a handful, straightened them out and pounded them right in. He kept right on that way till he had shingled almost half of the south side of the house. By now the sun was up and it was just starting to move towards the west so it was striking the south side of the house. That was when Grampa Jesse figured he would go on in and

21

have some breakfast before he finished the job off. As he was going in, though, he noticed something that was sort of strange. A whole flock of robins was just sitting there on that lawn and a-looking up at those shingles he'd just nailed. No accounting for how a bird will act, he thought, then went on in.

Grama Bowman had heard him pounding for the last hour or so and she had his breakfast ready. The usual menu, about five pounds of bacon, ten gallons of coffee, a gross or so of pancakes and enough maple syrup to drown a cat in. The Bowmans always liked their maple syrup. Grampa Jesse used to tell about Uncle Forrest Bowman who had a great liking for maple syrup but would never use a napkin on account of the fact he had a full face beard. Every spring they would shave that beard off him, boil it down and get exactly twenty-eight quarts of high-grade maple syrup.

When Grampa Jesse had just about finished that breakfast of his he said to Grama Bowman, "Go on out and see what I done." He was about as proud as a peacock about all he'd accomplished before he even sat down for his pancakes. But Grama Bowman wasn't outside for more than a minute before she came back in.

"Well," she said, "those shingles don't look half bad. But when are you going to put them up?"

"Put 'em up?" he said. "I already done one whole side of the house,"

"Not that I can see," she said.

Grampa Jesse put down his favorite coffee cup, the cracked one with the chipped handle that was still perfectly good. He walked outside and there he saw a sight that made him feel to low he would have needed stilts to scratch a snake's back. Those shingles were all laying on the ground, every whichaway. There was just one single solitary shingle left on the house, hanging by a single nail and the strange thing is that a robin was flapping around it. Even stranger, though, was what that nail was doing. It was wiggling and dodging as that robin dove at it. As Grampa Jesse watched that nail wiggled itself free of the shingle, fell to the ground, and crawled into its hole before the robin could get it. That was when Grampa Jesse realized what he had done. That frost had come so fast the night before that it had stiffened up the night crawlers on his lawn. With those old glasses of his he hadn't know the difference and he'd picked up and nailed those shingles on with frozen worms!

"Grandpa Jesse and the Used Nails" dances along the border between credibility and incredibility. Bruchac first establishes Grandpa Jesse's character: he is so absent-minded that he reminds us of the old European numskull characters who were revived in the 1950's as "The Little Moron." A typical thrifty Yorker, he saved things. Without any shift in syntax, Bru-

23

chac slips into that world of rigid-but-absurd logic which is home to so many tall tales: Grandpa is defying the laws of gravity for a prized hammer. Bruchac sets us up again, compounding authentic particulars about the acquisition of the shingles and the nails, building facts and details right to that passing mention of the breakfast for a giant. One more moment of credibility, and the logic simply explodes.

Harvey Carr

HI JOHN, TALL TALES AND
HAPPY TRAILS. THAT'S ME.

Harvey

Harvey Carr was born in Watson, Saskatchewan, in 1917. His father was a native of Otsego County, New York; his mother of Southern Ontario. Two of Harvey's grandparents were English and Irish; one was Scots and Dutch, and one was Irish. Harvey Carr's father ran "a sort of U-Haul with horses . . ." where Ontario farmers could exchange a cumbersome ox team and wagon for a more town-manageable horse and buggy or — in winter — a cutter. Carr's father also worked in the woods. As soon as he was old enough, Harvey, who claims to be "the only one in the family who didn't have a brother . . ." went along with his father "to watch."

When he was twelve, Harvey's family moved to Otsego County, which he describes as "a very depressed area . . . but we didn't know it." Carr observes that people today complain about not being able to afford a color TV. "We were so poor we only had black and white *crayons!* There was nothing to distract you . . . not a lot to do except homemade entertainment. The funny thing is that morale was higher than it is today. We appreciated what we had. People were happy . . . We had square dances in some-body's dining room. It's be snowin' and blowin' and roads driftin' shut. We didn't worry about it."

As a woodsman, Carr "bounced around wherever there was trees." He has worked in many of the Adirondack live-in lumber camps, including one where the men walked more than eight miles to get into camp. He worked as an Adirondack guide until he decided "he liked the hunt and fish too much to spoil it by guiding."

After four and a half years as a paratrooper in the 101st Airborne, Harvey Carr was hired by the Tree Preservation Company. By the time of his retirement, twenty-three years later, he was manager of crews for New York State. Carr lives in Blue Mountain Lake with his wife of nearly fifty years. He teaches fishing classes to children at the local arts center, and serves as

27

chairman of the Board of Fire Commissioners. When the Hochschield family was establishing the Adirondack Museum, it was Harvey who brought the cabin of Noah John Rondeau, the famous Adirondack hermit, out of the woods and set it up at the museum.

Harvey can be found every morning, drinking coffee at the local convenience store, whittling trick chains, stretching the ordinary and shrinking the fabulous with his friends — as they did in the lumber camps, as the western Saskatchewan farmers did in his father's livery.

ZUCCHINI CANOE

I had quite a good garden here last year. Now the zucchini, once that starts growing the only way you can stop it is to shoot it! It really grows. We had one last year and it kept growing and growing. It got to be three foot long and about a foot in diameter, almost like watermelon. It was too big to eat and I said, "I wonder what I'm goin' to do with that thing!"

So I left it. Well, it grew and it grew and it kept growin'. It got up to be eleven, twelve feet long. It was quite an oddity and people looked at it and said "What're you goin' to do with it?" Then I decided to make a dugout canoe out of it.

I hollowed it all out, took the seeds and all the insides out of it and dried it up some. Then I got down to the lake and put it in the water and it floated pretty good. It seemed pretty stable. I took along a couple of paddles, in case I lost one, and I was paddlin' over and I got into West Bay. I looked and here come a beaver. I said, "Well, that's nice." I always like to see wildlife. He was swimmin' around and he come up right next to the boat and I thought that was pretty cute. He sniffed at the side of the boat and he took a bite out of it!

He went back, ten twelve feet away from the boat—I guess so he wouldn't splash me—and he swatted his tail on the water, the way a beaver does. Sounds just like a rifle shot. Here came seven or eight more beaver. Well, they ate that canoe right out from under me and I had to swim to shore!

This year I got another comin' along good. It's only about seven feet long, still growin'. I'm going to try it again, make another canoe. I think what I can do is I got two alternatives. I can put a twenty five horse motor on it and I can outrun the beaver. Or maybe I'll fiberglass it. I haven't decided which one to do yet.

They're pretty clever little things, in some ways, them beaver. I was cutting logs up on Dun Brook Mountain and ever night when I got through cuttin, I'd fill up the saw with gas and oil for the chain and get it all ready for the next morning. Next mornin', just a couple of cranks and away it would go.

So, one mornin' I went up and cranked two or three times and it wouldn't go. I cranked and I cranked and it wouldn't go. I checked it over and the gas tank was empty. "Well," I said, "I guess I fergot to fill it last night." So I filled it up, worked perfect all day. I said, "Well, tonight I'm going to make sure I fill that!" I filled it up with gas and oil and next mornin' I came back and I cranked and cranked and the same thing! Gas tank was empty.

Well, it must be a hole in the gas line or the carburetor was leakin'. I checked it all over and couldn't find nothin' that was wrong with it. It's run all day — run good after I filled it up!

One night I filled it up and went down to camp. But when I got there I still had a little daylight left so I thought I'd go back up and check that saw and see where it was leakin'. Well, I got halfway up the mountain and I heard this chain saw runnin'. Sounded like mine! Nobody else had a chainsaw up there anyway. So I tippy-toed up kind of careful and there was these two beaver. They was using that saw to cut timber and buildin' a dam. Boy, they were havin' a field day!

One of my buddies here in town, I told him about it and he said, "Boy, them beaver are pretty smart little animals, aren't they?"

"Not really," I said. "I think they're a couple of dumb ones up there."

"Whaddaya mean dumb?"

I said, "Well, there was five gallon of gas and a gallon of chain oil there and if they'd of just filled that saw back up when they got through with it, I never would of caught 'em."

HIBERNATING WITH THE BEAR

I like to hunt and fish around here and I had quite an experience last fall. I was deer hunting, a-tippy-toeing along over Blue Ridge country here and all of a sudden I dropped right down into the ground. Dropped my rifle. Guess what it was was a crevice in between the rocks and I fell right down in, all twenty or twenty-five feet. When I hit, I heard a little "whoof!" of some kind. It jarred me some and I was catching my breath and I looked around and there was a big black bear sound asleep, hibernatin'.

I said to myself, "Boy, I'm in a problem now, quite a problem!" He was in between me and the mouth of the tunnel where he came in and I didn't want to try to crawl over him. If he'd woke up, he'd of torn me right to pieces, I guess. So I said, "Oh, I guess I might as well take a nap anyway." So I went to sleep.

Well, I'd sleep for two or three days and wake up and take a look and old bear was sleepin', so wasn't much else I could do and I slept again. And every time I'd wake up and check, old bear was still there. It went on like that till about the first of April, I guess. That was when I woke up one day and I looked and the bear was gone! I figured I'd better get out of there, too. I was pretty hungry. It'd been from November till April. So, I tip-toed out through the tunnel.

I thought I'd stop off at the neighbors' house and get something to eat. But as hungry as I was, I'd make a pig of myself and eat everything in the house. I'd better go to the supermarket. The nearest supermarket was down in Indian Lake. The Grand Union. They got one of them rubber mats, you know, in front of the door. You step on that and your weight trips the switch and it opens the door. Well, when I got there and stepped on that mat I'd lost so much weight that the doggone door wouldn't open! I had to stand there and wait until another customer stood on there with me before the door would open.

I don't know if I paid all that bill for what I ate yet or not.

BRUNO, THE BEAR

Well, I got hold of this bear cub and I trained him. He grew up to a pretty good size, about three hundred pounds. I trained him and he'd do pretty much what I said and I could ride on his back.

Every payday I'd take him down to our little local bar, have my little party and ride him home. He'd lay down in the flower bed outside and I'd go in and get him a couple of soda pops and a candy bar or two. I didn't want to give him any beer. I couldn't take him inside anyway. There was this sign on the door says NO BARE FEET and he had four of 'em. Anyhow, he'd lay there and wait for me and drink that soda pop.

I come out one night pretty tipsy. I just patted him one and said, "Come on, Bruno." And he snarled at me! I said "Bruno, what's the matter with you?" I didn't know what was wrong. I cuffed him once and he snapped at me! Well, we had quite a hassle there. I had to slap him up pretty good and finally he tamed down and I hopped on his back and everything worked good. Came up to the house, got to the back door and there lay Bruno, sound asleep! I was on the wrong bear!

In "The Zucchini Canoe," Carr parlays an annual gardener's dilemma into a stretch tale of Yankee ingenuity. Unlike many tall tales, which begin and end with an ordinary-seeming narrative, this story begins with the logical extension of an absurd premise. A factual account of the sort often shared among rural men serves as the middle section. Spinning out his woes about the chain saw, Carr fools the listener into thinking the fun is over. As he builds to the climax, the deliciously rigid assigning of human traits to beavers, Carr employs what Gilbert Ryle calls the category mistake. *Carolyn S. Brown in* The Tall Tale in American Folklore and Literature *(Knoxville: University of Tennessee Press, 1987) presents many clear examples of this device, which ". . . creates an absurdity by allocating an object or concept to a logical type or category to which it does not belong."*

The tall tale hero is a comic protagonist who survives in a dangerous, often cruel universe through, according to Suzanne Langer, ". . .wit, luck, . . . or philosophical acceptance of mischance." (Suzanne Langer. "The Comic Rhythm" in Feeling and Form. *New York: Charles Scribners' Sons, 1953.) Northrup Frye adds that the comic protaganist is ". . . opportunity fraught with mischance." (Northrup Frye. "The Mythos of Spring: Comedy" in* The Anatomy of Criticism. *Princeton: Princeton University Press, 1957.) He is "pure life force." In "Hibernating with the Bear," Carr uses the category mistake again, this time to show a hero who survives because he adapts. The results are, again, the logical extension of an absurd first premise. In "Bruno, the Bear," the narrator comes through what in stage comedy would be called* comic doubling *by means of an extraordinary strength treated as absolutely commonplace. One is reminded of Davy Crockett and the alligator wrestle.*

Chris Morley

Maurice "Chris" Morley is a descendent of the first permanent settler of Saratoga Springs, Alex Bryan, and of an immigrant Irish lacemaker and tailor who settled in Greenwich, Washington County. His grandfather Morley's tailor shop in Greenwich was a local gathering place where his grandfather "sat cross-legged on the table and the guys came in to talk."

At age ten—"I just beat the child labor laws"—Morley became a messenger for the D&H Railroad. (He is proud that, at age fifteen, he was the youngest person to hold a five-year pass, good for rail travel anywhere in the United States.) "The way things fell," muses Morley, "you take a job if you can get it. You do it if you have a chance." He has worked as a "mule spinner" in a yarn mill; as boss of the picking room and on the carding machine in a woolen mill,; as a first-class armor welder for American Locomotive Company; as a dairy farmer, a driller, a blaster, a fitter, a grinder, and a theatre usher. Morley was aboard the carrier *Essex* when she was commissioned. He finished his tour of duty in the Marine Corps as the Admiral's body guard. "I was," he says, "the only one who had to be all slicked up to go on duty."

Morley retired from thirty-two years in construction to be a mainstay volunteer at the Saratoga Museum, where he maintains a toy shop, impersonates an Irish immigrant for interpretation of certain events, and presides over the smoke house he constructed.

His stories "go back 130 or 140 years. Civil War veterans used to hang around the station, telling stories about Ballston before the Civil War," while young Chris was waiting for dispatches. "I had to sit in the corner and keep still: I was only a kid." A Swedish man who ran an apple storage across from the station gave Morley a jacknife and an apple crate, "and told me to start whittlin'." In his retirement, Morley makes wooden toys which remind him of incidents from his boyhood and provide him with the opportunity to recount those stories.

41

I WONDER HOW THAT
BEER TASTED

Back in the days of the Depression, I went to work for the D&H Railroad as a messenger boy. I was about ten years old and used to run around delivering telegrams and messages to the mills in town.

I'd often sit in the corner of the station listening to the old timers, some of whom were Civil War veterans and they'd be telling war stories and jokes, lots of jokes. Some of those jokes might not have been funny at the time, but looking back on them, you couldn't help but laugh.

There were these two fellows who worked in the stable of the old Lincoln Hotel. They liked to drink and they didn't like to do much work. They'd wash down the horses and then take the money and buy beer.

On one slow day, with no money in hand, one of the men said to the other, "Go get that horse sponge and wring it out well." They pushed that sponge down into a crock and took it round to one of the taverns to have it filled. After it was full, they turned their pockets out but they couldn't produce a dime. No money, No Beer was the motto of the day and the barkeeper dumped the brew back into the barrel and handed them back their crock.

When they got back to the stable, they broke the crock, took out that sponge, wrung out its contents and drank it down.

I suppose it must have happened that way, but I can't help but wonder how that beer tasted!

TWO STORIES FROM ANTIOCH HILL

I want to tell you about a dry season we had, up in my neck of the woods. Up in the foothills of the Antioch hill, there's a small settlement. Things had been real dry for pretty near a whole year. There hadn't been much snow and things was dried out pretty bad. When this great fire started in our little hamlet and was burning down the feed store, the line went out and everybody rushed in to help. We didn't have much water to put it out so we was using brooms and throwing dirt on. But that fire was spreading and it looked like the whole little town would burn.

Up on top of Antioch Mountain, there's a family known as the Veeders. Well, things were so poor up there that the biggest crop Ma and Pa Veeder could raise was kids. The fire was ragin' away and we happened to look up and down the mountain comes Pa and Ma Veeder and all their kids in their old truck. My Gosh, we couldn't believe it because they drove right into the middle of the fire. Pa Veeder yelled, "Kids, take your jackets and beat out that fire."

They got out of that truck and stomped and beated and bammed and whammed and pretty soon, the fire was out. My Gosh, we couldn't believe it. They'd helped save our little hamlet. So somebody took a hat and passed it around and they took up a collection. There was nine dollars and eighty-eight cents. We gave it to Pa Veeder.

Somebody in the crowd said, "Hey, Pop, what you goin' to do with all that money?"

He said, "Well, it is quite a sum. But the first thing I think I'll do is get the brakes on this darn truck fixed!"

Quite a few things happen around Antioch Hill, even if it is a little place. Just recently, we lost our minister. We couldn't afford to pay him too much — we gave him a few bushels of potatoes, some corn and a little cash. But he got a better offer, so he left.

So we all got together and we decided and we sent word and they sent us another minister. This past Sunday he come to do a little preachin' to see if we liked him. So we all got on our best bib overalls with the fronts on and we got all sharped up and got all the kids together and we marched down to church. Well, he was some preacher! My gosh, he preached for pretty near two hours! Finally he gave up and we all shook his hand at the door and went on our way.

Well, the preacher went out to get on his horse and found that the horse had thrown a shoe. So he asked around. He says, "Do we have a blacksmith?"

46

"Yes, we have a blacksmith."

"Oh, then I can get this horse reshoed so I can get on my way."

"Well, you won't be able today because the blacksmith doesn't work on Sunday."

So the first thing Monday morning he took the horse on over to the blacksmith and said the horse needed a shoe. The blacksmith said "Yes," and he reached up and got a piece of brand-new iron and put it in the furnace and got it nice and hot and started bangin' out a shoe.

The preacher was lookin' at him and lookin' at him and he says to himself, "My gosh, the work he's doin' on this, this is gonna cost me a fortune. I don't know what I'm going to do."

So he says, "Say, you know, I'm nothin' but a poor preacher."

And the blacksmith had his hammer high in mid-air, ready to strike a blow upon the shoe and he stopped in mid-air and turned and looked at the preacher and said, "Yes, I know. I listened to you for two hours last Sunday!"

Chris Morley is the teller of the true tall tale. Although his stories contain the occasional localized traveling motif, he is what Richard Dorson calls a sagaman. *(Bloodstoppers and Bearwalkers: Folk Traditions of the Upper Peninsula.* Cambridge and London: Harvard University Press, 1952.*) Sagamen, Dorson says, are "gifted with talk beyond their fellows." Morley's stories and anecdotes of local charac-*

ters are almost-true. The heroes are tricksters and punsters — amoral, comic "little guys," who survive through luck, wit, and chance. Morley's narratives assume a close community whose values are taken for granted, where a fire means that people rally to help and where Sunday means that people go to church.

Larry Morrison

Larry Morrison was born in Montgomery County just at the beginning of World War I. After high school, he worked as a salesman for Beechnut, where he advanced to the position of agricultural purchasing. Morrison was with Beechnut for forty-two years. "We retired and went to Carolina and finally moved back up this way — don't ask me why!"

Morrison, who says he "generally tells the truth," is master of the quick response and the untoppable pun. He and his wife, Ruth, celebrated their 50th wedding anniversary in August 1989. "It was a roast, not a celebration," he comments. "It's love backwards."

It is true, as he claims in his saga of whittlers and carvers, that Larry Morrison is an accomplished carver of life-like birds. But he is also accomplished at colorful depictions in words. I'm still thinking about the one he told of the politician who was "so crooked that, when he died, his friends had to screw him into the ground to bury him."

CARVING HORSE HEADS

I'm a whittler and a bird carver. I attribute my woodworking skills to Irish relatives on my mother's side. My Uncle Jimmy was quite a whittler and a carver. My cousin, who's a tail gunner on a bakery truck in Belfast, sent me some carving knives after my uncle's death. My Uncle Jimmy was quite a talent, you know. One of his works was quite famous. It was a portrait he did, called it a study in black and grey. It was, of course, "Whittler's Mother" by James McNeill Whittler.

Folks love to gather around whittlers when they work. Their interest is in seeing how much blood will be drawn from those sharp knives. Not having any blood myself, I took up story-telling to keep them amused.

Now recently, I got this contract to carve wooden horse heads. It isn't exactly a contract. It seems I got word that there was quite a shortage of horse's heads down in Washington, D.C. and so I thought there would be quite a market for them. And I carved up quite a number of them.

It turned out, however, that it wasn't that there was a shortage of horse's heads after all. What it is, is that with the people who have been sent down there in the government in recent years it is just that we have a surplus of the other end of the horse.

Elliot Older

"Oh, Elliot, I just tripped over the baby gate. I think I broke my toe. Can I call you back?"

"Were you carryin' anything?"

Elliott Older is a very funny man, but you'll miss the dry, wry understatements if you aren't quick. Elliott likes to talk; he likes people. He has a quiet, unsurpassed eye for contradiction and absurdity. The youngest son of a woods family, Elliot grew up in the lumber camps and settlements around Lake Desolation, Saratoga County. His mother was a lumbercamp cook. His father and his stepfather were skilled woodsmen. It was a situation where quick wit and a sense of irony were survival tools. It was a culture of raconteurs, where good talk was valued as the chief form of entertainment. Both Older parents sang songs handed down in the family since sometime before their eighteenth century migration to Saratoga County from England. His father, Ben Older, was a maker of local song parodies. Elliott, who also loves and sings the old traditional songs, is at his best in a tale swap, where his modest bearing gives lie to his store of traditional tall tales and his agile, unstudied comic timing.

Elliott lives in Middle Grove with Enid, his wife of fifty-five years. He is a member of the Odd Fellow Lodge and of the Middle Grove United Methodist Church. In addition to his skill as a talker, Elliot is accomplished in cabinetry. He is a serious collector of old Saratoga County tools and he is an avid student of local history.

THE WOODCHOPPER'S CRUISE

I was thinking the other day about some of the woodchoppers I worked in the camp with. First of all, there was these two I knew. They wasn't the intellectual type. But then you didn't get the intellectual type working in the woods. These two'd worked all winter and they'd saved up quite a bundle, so they decided to go into town and have some fun. Well, as soon as they got there they saw this sign. It said: Ferry Cruise: $75.

One of them said, "Now that sounds interesting. Why don't we go. We ain't got nothing else to do." He wanted to see something, you know. The other one he agreed and so they went inside. Well, as soon as they got in there, the guys beat 'em up, took their money, tied them onto two planks and put 'em on the river, the both of them.

As they're going down the river, the first one catches up to the other one and he says, "Do you suppose they serve liquor on this cruise?"

"I don't know," said the other one. "They didn't last year."

Now there was this other woodchopper I knew. It seems we were having a woodchopper's dance. This one young lad come over to my house and he said, "Gee, Elliot, my collar's awful tight."

I looked at him and I said, "Well, no wonder, you've got your head through the buttonhole."

Then I looked down at his feet and he had a white shoe and a black one on. They was both brand new. I said to him, "Where'd you get that pair of shoes? They don't match."

"Well, that's right," he said," and you know, I got another pair at home just like these."

Most all of your woodchopper and teamsters were quite big drinkers. This one day this guy took a load out at the lake and got pretty drunk out to Harwoods and came back in layin' in the box of the wagon. So the boys they unhooked his team and they left him right there.

The next morning he woke up and said, "Boy, I've either lost a damn good team or found a damn good wagon!"

LION

Thinking of lying, there was this little boy who was just an awful liar. So his father decided he would do something about it. They had a big collie dog and the father took that dog and trimmed it so that it looked like a lion. Then he let it out. Pretty soon, that little boy came in.

"Paw, there's a lion outside and it's been killing everybody."

"Now," his father said. "That's a lie. That wasn't no lion. That was just our collie dog. I want you to go up to your room and talk to God and tell him you're sorry for all those lies you've been telling."

Well, that little boy went up to his room, but before too long he come right back down.

"Paw," he said. "I been talking to God and he thought that dog was a lion, too."

HOWARD NEHR'S TEAM OF OXEN AND THE OAK LOG

Gettin' in to camp was important late in the afternoon when the sun starts goin' down. It's the big woods and the shadows come over fast and everybody, of course, they're done for the day and they want to get into camp — a hot supper and everything. Howard Nehr was doin' some skiddin' with a yoke of oxen. The cook had told him when he went out in the mornin' if he seed somethin' good in the line of dry hardwood to bring it into camp. Durin' the day he did spot a big oak log. Must have been two foot in diameter or better and maybe sixteen feet long and well seasoned.

He said, "Well, I'll take that back to camp tonight."

So when they quit he come along with his oxen and he drove the skiddin' hook into the end of the log. And then he was tired so he sat down on the end of the log and he rested his back on the log and he hollered "GIT!" And away they went.

Well, he fell asleep thinkin' about a hot supper and I'll be into camp in pretty quick time. He woke up and it's all quiet and dark and he could see stars overhead. He got up and he was still right where he'd laid down! He got down off the bark to look at the end of the log and there wasn't any log there. When he'd hollered the oxen had jumped and twitched it right out of the bark. And they'd gone right on to camp. And Howard still had to walk in and get a cold supper.

"The Woodchoppers' Cruise" adapts an old-world numskull motif to a local setting. "Lion" is a joke in the guise of a tall tale. Many other stories in Elliot Older's repertoire are elaborations of very old European travelling tall tale motifs. At least one, a story about a drunk woodchopper who answers his jug, can be found, in slightly different form, in Greek New Comedy!

Lawrence Older

Hunger for music, a sense of the importance of local stories, and a certain dramatic flair seem to be in the Older family blood. **Lawrence Older**'s grandfather is said to have mounted the crossbeam at a local barn-raising and to have sung for four hours. His sister, Edith, walked all the way across the mountain from Lake Desolation — at night — to get a fourth string for her fiddle. Former employees of the Ballston Knitting Mill remember that Edith and another sister, Evelyn, sang in harmony as they worked. Lawrence's oldest brother, Ben, had a large repertoire of British ballads and woods songs. Lawrence remembers, at the age of six or seven, settling a fight with a boy from a neighboring farm in exchange for a new song. At four, he sat outside the dance hall in Lake Desolation, listening to the music, crying, and promising himself that, someday, he would play the fiddle.

Lawrence's stories were more than entertainment: they were pieces of a world he was determined to keep alive. He made the rounds weekly of his adopted children and designated artistic heirs, compelled to teach the stories, and the songs he had learned from his family — and from anyone who would teach him — to *anyone* who would learn them. A man whose formal education ended at sixth grade, and who went to work in the woods at age fourteen, Lawrence Older was a born teacher, a master tradition bearer.

Older appeared in many major folk festivals and in many college folklore classrooms. Among his favorites were the Newport Folk Festival, the Smithsonian Festival of American Folklore, the Niskayuna Festival, the Fox Hollow Festival, and the prestigious Pinewoods Camp, run by the Country Dance and Song Society of America, At his death in 1982, at the age of 70, Lawrence Older was a nominee for the nation's highest honor for a traditional artist: The National Endowment for the Arts Heritage Award.

THE MAN FROM VERMONT AND THE BASS VIOL

Now there was this man from Vermont. I should tell you that I used to tell this story and I'd say, "There was a man from Delaware" and everybody would look back and everything would always go flat. Then I just happened to say " A man from Vermont" one time and the whole hall just laughed their head off. I don't have to be hit in the head with a hammer to get a message. So ever since then, it's been a man from Vermont.

This man from Vermont, he was a pokey old cuss. He'd come in to have his supper and when his wife was all through eating and he'd still be picking away at his plate. When his wife was all washed up, he'd still be settin' there. One day, though, he went to an auction and he picked up a bass viol. He brought it home and it just transformed him. Every night he'd bolt his supper down just as fast as he could and he'd get in that Sittin' Room and he'd get that thing out and get it down between his legs and tighten the bow and he'd start, just playing the same note. And he'd play that same note again and again. That went on for weeks. His wife was patient, figuring he'd move on to another note sooner or later. One night, she finally broke down and she said, "Ethan?"

"Ayup?"

"Did you ever hear anyone play a bass viol?"

"Lots of people."

She said, "Didn't you notice they run their fingers up and down."

He said, "They was still looking for their place. I found mine!"

PAT MALONE AND THE OX

John Collins used to live around here and one night after I sang "Pat Malone," he come up after the show and said "You know, Pat Malone used to work around here," and he told me this story.

Pat Malone had a yoke of oxen and he come up and he drew logs from the big doubleheader up to the bankin' grounds. One day, it'd been such a hard day on the oxen that on the way back to camp, one of 'em give out and fell right on the road. Pat wanted to get back to camp and of course the other ox did too, so he got under the yoke where the one ox had fallen, stepped over the ox and started down the road with that yoke on his shoulders. Just then, the other ox started to run away. Well, Pat he had to keep up with it, and he started hollerin'.

The men down the road goin' in from chopping, they heard the hollerin' and yellin' and looked up the road and saw the runaway coming. Well they got across the road and formed a human chain to get that ox stopped.

71

One of the men, he broke out of the chain and run right up and grabbed on to Pat Malone.

Pat said, "I'LL STAND, just hold onto that damn ox!"

JIM'S BOOT

Now Jim was this old man who lived next to us and after he retired from the lumber camps he just went to seed. Us kids, though, was about the only ones who could tolerate him and we always went next door to see him because he had two real good songs that he'd sing.

I want to tell you a story about Jim one of the last winters he was working in the big woods in the lumber camp. Mother was cookin' in there and Jim was blacksmith. He hadn't had his boots off all winter. Well, folks generally wouldn't take their boots off unless somethin' happened. Along about February there in the room where the men sat around, we called it the Ram's Pasture, Jim started movin' his foot in his boot. Of course that was a form of entertainment. It had been quiet up till then and there he was studyin' his toe. When he became aware that they was watchin' him, he cut it out. That was around Monday night. Wednesday night he did the same thing and he done it a little longer. And everybody was just watchin' that boot. Friday night, he'd waited about as long as he could and he started to unlace that boot. By the time he'd got that boot unlaced, John Phillip Sousa and his band could have come in and nobody would have paid no attention at all because everybody wanted to see what was goin' to happen.

When Jim slid that boot off, all he had left there was a little bit of heel and no foot! He studied it a bit and then he said to himself, "There, that darn thing's been gone for two weeks and I knew it!"

That was our entertainment!

BILL GREENFIELD AND THE TWIN LAMBS

Bill Greenfield used to tell about the old man that came to Arnold's. These old people were entertaining and they didn't want to work or do anything useful. While they were at your place they'd sing in the evenings or tell stories. That was the only time kids could stay up late. And this old man came to Arnold's every year on his visit and he'd tell about what a great trapper he'd been in the old days.

He'd make those stories so exciting that young Bill said "Boy, oh boy, oh boy, I'd like to see a bear caught in a trap one time and killed."

So the old man sez, "Well, if I had a way," he said, "I'd do it for you."

And Mr. Arnold said, "Well we got a muzzle loader here and we got bear traps, everything the same as it used to be in the old days any fall you want to try it."

So this particular fall, the old man and Bill Greenfield, who was a young lad, they went up on the mountain back of there. This is in Oak Valley. And they built a little log pen and then they went back to the farm and they got a ewe, a female sheep, for bait. Bears like sheep to eat. They put this ewe in the pen and some

76

hay and some water and they set bear traps on all four corners. They went up every morning to look at the traps and they got up there this one morning and there was a bear in the trap. The old man was so excited, he'd got the gun loaded right, he run right up and he pulled off and he shot that bear and he went right over. It was killed for all intents and purposes, but it still had struggle left in it. The old man got too excited and he gets up close and the bear rakes out like that and he rakes that old man's intestines right out!

Young Bill Greenfield was a fast-thinkin' kid. He didn't try to save anything that was torn out of the old man cause it was just scattered here and there. He jumped right over into the pen and he butchered that ewe and took her intestines right out clean and he put them in the old man and sews him up with hay wire that was holdin' the traps, you see. Outside of a little soreness, the old man recovered.

Best of all, next spring he had twin lambs!

"Howard Nehr's Team of Oxen and the Oak Log" is a skillful, single-motif elaboration of a tall tale conceit, *or the absurd disregard for the nature of a material object (Brown. The Tall Tale). This is an example of a narrative which would separate insiders, who know that logs don't "twitch right out of the bark," from outsiders, who might fall for the ruse. It is, as Constance Rourke observes, the inversion of*

*the city slicker / country rube jokes popular
after the Civil War. (Constance Rourke.* American Humor: A Study of the National Character. *1931; reprint, New York: Harcourt, Brace,
Jovanovich, 1959.) These jokes, perhaps
reflecting the defeat of the agrarian South by
the industrial North, spawned many retalia-
tory oral narratives about the clever country
person, pretending to be stupid at the city slicker's expense. Howard Nehr's team of oxen with
their log are close cousins to the jokes in the
well-known "Arkansas Traveler."*

*Lawrence Older loved jokes like "The Man
from Vermont and the Bass Viol," which actu-
ally were little character sketches. He must
have known hundreds of them. Characteristi-
cally, he would chuckle to himself and echo the
last part of the punch line: " 'I found mine!'
See?"*

Frame story *is the term applied to the tech-
nique of telling a story which was told to the
narrator by someone else. By setting "Pat
Malone and the Ox" in such a frame, Older
distances himself from the incident, a tech-
nique particularly appropriate for an account
of a strong man of mythic proportions. The
exaggeration by understatement in the punch
line is characteristic of tall tale humor.*

*Maddie Older, Lawrence and Elliot's
mother, was, in fact, a lumber camp cook.
Both Lawrence and Elliot remember winters so
cold that their mother's perspiration from
standing over the stove would freeze her hair*

on the side of her head away from the heat. When the truth itself is an exaggeration, stretching — or shrinking — that truth for entertainment seems natural. The Ram's Pasture, *the Older family name for the room in the bunkhouse where the men sat around, is a brilliant imbedded metaphor, suggesting a vignette of woodsmen cooped up — and acting up! It is the setting for "Jim's Boot," a masterpiece of exaggeration through understatement, which manages to convey a good bit of the texture of life in the bunkhouse with considerable economy.*

Bill Greenfield is a Saratoga County descendant of the soldier braggarts in Plautus and Aristophanes, and an heir to the exaggerated accounts of America's first tall tale tellers, Benjamin Franklin and Baron Munchhausen. (Benjamin Franklin. Benjamin Franklin's Letters to the Press, 1757–1775. *Ed. Verner W. Crance. Chapel Hill: University of North Carolina Press, 1950. Raspe, R. E.* et al. Singular Travels, Campaigns, and Adventures of Baron Munchhausen. *Ed. and intro. John Carswell. 1948; reprint New York: Dover, 1960.) Bill Greenfield was born in 1833 in Edinburgh, New York, the grandson of Scottish immigrants to the new republic. Apparently, Bill was a practical joker and trickster who made himself the hero of the classic European tall tales, which had wide circulation in the colonies in the eighteenth century. Bill continued to tell the tales his father, Abner Green, told, elabo-*

79

rating a bit as he did. The tales passed into tradition in northern Saratoga County, where they were collected by Harold Thompson's students in the 1930's and 1940's. (Body, Boots, and Britches: Folktales, Ballads, and Speech from Country New York. *New York: Dover, 1939, 1967). Greenfield is buried in Clark Cemetery, near Northville, Saratoga County. Stories about Bill Greenfield, and stories attributed to him, still circulate among local residents. "Bill Greenfield and the Twin Lambs" is an extraordinary mix of what Carolyn Brown calls the* grotesque tall tale, *which combines laughter and revulsion, and the magic outcome one expects in fairy tales.*

Dick Richards

Love & Kisses to Jean

Dick Gilchrist

Clarence "Daddy Dick" Richards' father, a woodsman, musician, and vaudeville entertainer, started his son playing fiddle at age nine. Young Richards was so quick that, by the age of twelve, he was playing for local dances and substituting for the caller when necessary. He was also a song-sponge: Bradley Kincaid, the early radio personality, had a summer home in Stafford's Bridge, Saratoga County. Kincaid had a standing agreement with the boy that Kincaid would give young Richards a chicken for every song Kincaid hadn't heard. "Most every Saturday," Dick says, "I'd ride home across the mountain with two chickens hanging from the handlebars of my bicycle." He was already an accomplished musician when he lost his left hand in a paper mill accident in 1936, having played with his father and uncle for square dances and house parties for about six years. Within six months of the accident, he had discovered a way to continue playing the fiddle, and, three months after that, he won a fiddling contest!

Dick was a regular at area dude ranches and an early entertainer on Radio WGY in Schenectady, New York. In the 1940's, he produced a record of traditional square dance calls for Decca Records. He has appeared in educational and commercial films, and on television. He has performed with many top country and bluegrass stars, including Washington County's country music legend, Smokey Greene. It was Smokey who gave him the nickname "Daddy Dick." Richards is generous in his charitable appearances, especially as a member of his Shriners' band, the "Oriental Hillbillies."

As Frontiertown's Davy Crockett, Dick Richards is the only known person to have received a ticket for parking a stage coach illegally in the village of Lake George—and that *is* the truth. He has also been known, in his finer moments with Smokey Greene, to produce—alive, on stage, at midnight—a six-foot man-eating chicken! (Smokey Greene is six feet tall.

Richards handed him a piece of fried chicken and said, "Smokey, start eatin'. Ladies and Gentlemen, just as we advertised last week, here, at midnight, is a *six foot man — eatin' chicken*.") There is reason to think that Dick Richards may well be the next Bill Greenfield, the person to whom tall tale motifs are attached for generations to come.

In 1988, "Daddy Dick" Richards was named a Master Artist by the Folk Arts Program of the New York State Council of the Arts for his preservation and perpetuation of Adirondack music, song, and narrative traditions.

THE ICEBERG FEVER

I don't exactly know how I got mixed up with these fellas here telling all these tall tales cuz I want you to know right now that I never told a lie in my life. I've been married for over forty years and I have learned to stretch the truth a little bit. But as far as bein' a downright liar, I wouldn't do a thing like that. I always tell the truth, even if I have to lie to do it!

It's days like this that remind me of how cold it gets up here in this territory that I live in. I can remember one particular night that it got so cold the smoke froze right in the chimney and we had to bring the chimney into the house to thaw it out before we could get the fire to burn. Now to get a fire to burn, of course you have to light a match to start the fire. And it's so cold up here in this territory that the flame'll freeze right on a match. You can't start a fire with that. All you get is light. It's a good thing to have a lot of night on a cold night like that, but you gotta have some heat from somewhere. So the best thing to do is rub two sticks together in the stove and when the sparks begin to fly they get that stove to burning.

It's been so cold around here that I've been told people can look right out in their dooryard

and see chickens out there with their feathers held so tight to them they would smoke. Other people have seen roosters out in their dooryards with a cape on.

It gets so cold up here that the sun will freeze right in the sky and we'll have daylight all night. And it's days like this make me think of the time I caught the Iceberg Fever. Now I'm sure you all know what the Iceberg Fever is. That's a case where your temperature goes down instead of up and you sweat frost. I had the cold chills continuously for over two months,. You'd set in a chair and be shaking so much that after a while that chair would be broken right down. In fact, that's how come my father built a new house.

What really I want to tell you folks about is my family. You see I come from a long line of lumber jacks. My great grandfather was a lumber jack and my grandfather was a lumber jack and my father was a lumber jack and, of course, everybody knows if you want to be smart and preserve the trees you don't cut fifty or sixty trees down a day, you only cut about twenty trees. That's why my father used to go to the woods day after day, year round barefooted. That was so he could count up to twenty and know when he cut the last tree. His feet got so tough that instead of using the ax to cut the limbs off the trees he'd just go along and give them a kick with his bare foot. Saved a lot of wear and tear on the blade of that ax.

I used to go in the woods with my dad. I

guess possibly you've heard the expression "riding the saw." Well, that's what they used to do with me. They tied me on one handle there on my cradle on one end of a saw that was about twelve foot long and they dragged that saw back and forth through the tree and it worked out real well. I enjoyed that very much riding back and forth on that saw. It had one drawback, however. I ate so much of that sawdust that bark started to grow on the side of my face and they had to shave me with an ax. That was even before I could walk.

Hugh Richards

The very Best

To Dean

Hugh

Hugh Richards was born in the Palmer Falls section of Corinth, Saratoga County, New York, in 1921. He is the youngest of four children. His mother, Della Reynolds Richards from Porter Corners, worked as a chambermaid in the big hotels in Saratoga, where she was reputed to have "sung half the day" as she did her work. His father played fiddle at local "kitchen hops." "My father was a hard worker," Richards comments, "he worked [at the paper mill] as a chipper man." Hugh Richards is retired from quality control at International Paper. He has always "wanted to do a job nobody else could do." His stories are the ones he heard from his father and from other men as he was growing up. Hugh lives with his wife, Shirley, across the road from his brother "Daddy Dick" Richards in Lake Luzerne, Warren County, New York.

PHIDEAU

By accident I raised a very odd acting dog. It was a French dog. Not a poodle, not a French poodle. Oh no! He came right from France. In fact, his name was Phideau. Well, I taught that dog to go get a stick. You could throw it anywhere. You could throw that dog over your shoulder, throw him between your legs. Course you had to throw the stick first.

Well, to make a long story short I spent a long time with that dog. He'd go get a stick, stones, tin cans, anything you would throw. I was planning on entering him in a duck contest where the dog would swim out in the water and get ahold of a duck and bring it back to shore and save ammunition. But I never got to do that. I was down by the water one time counting my change and I accidentally dropped a quarter in the water. That dog dove in the water and came back right up there to me with that quarter! I told that to another fella and he said, "I'd like to see that!" So we went down by the water and I threw a quarter out into the water and the dog jumped in and he come up with a fish.

"Well, where's my quarter," I said. I didn't want to lose my quarter. That dog made a few motions to give me the idea that maybe that quarter was inside the fish. So I cut that fish open and there a dime and a nickel inside. Well I drawed the dog's attention to this. "Hey," I said, "I don't want to be gypped like this!" So the dog jumped back in the water and he come up with another fish. I cut that one open and there was the other dime!

That dog turned out to be a pickerel hound. He wouldn't retrieve a duck, but he could just jump into the water and come up with a pickerel every time. He would smell the tracks where pickerel had been up on the banks walking around there. He tracked one a half a mile there down to the edge of a lake and stood there barking at the base of a tree. I thought that dog had gone berserk. But he was putting up such a fuss I said, "Well, I'll see what's up the tree, anyway." So I clumb up the tree and low and behold, right up there on one of those branches was a big turtle's nest. And right in that nest was a fifteen inch pickerel, fast asleep.

Hugh Richards' story about "Phideau" is a direct descendent of a long line of "stretchers" about smart hunting dogs. The fish with the amazing contents is the vestige of a bit of magic, a motif borrowed by early woodsmen from the remembered European cousin of the tall tale, the fairy tale.

"I Always Tell the Truth" plays with the danger of coping with the extreme cold of a northern winter. *The absurd application of the rules of freezing liquid to smoke and flame is another example of a* tall tale conceit *(See* Brown, Tall Tale.*). These exaggerations about natural aggravations and dangers were common among men of earlier generations in these woods (See Thompson.* Body, Boots, and Britches.*) Some of the lies about cold weather first appeared in print in Joseph Addison and Richard Steele's* Tattler, *which was published in England in the early 18th century and was widely read on this side of the Atlantic. Other tall tale conceits first appeared thousands of years ago, in the plays of the Greek comedian, Aristophanes, and in the works of the Roman playwrite, Plautus. The stories about the strong feet, and about being born with a beard, are attributed both to the giants of earlier European tales and to Paul Bunyan.*

William B. "Bill" Smith

Jean,
thanks for setting through these
lies in this hot building.

Bill Smith

Bill Smith grew up in the country near South Colton, Saint Lawrence County, New York, the youngest of ten children. His parents owned a small farm and his father worked in the woods while his mother and the rest of the family took care of the farm.

"We did things the old way," Smith relates, "with horses and hand tools to work with, cutting wood and pulp with a cross cut saw, hunting at a young age, fishing, trapping, learning country songs and stories from many of the older people of the area." It was during these years that he learned the basket-making crafts which would bring him acclaim in later life. As he explains, "Indians from Hogansburg (the St. Regis Reservation) came to our house and cut black ash trees and pounded them with a head axe, separating the annual rings to make them into pack baskets and clothing baskets. The women made sweet grass baskets. Being a small boy, I would follow them around, getting in the way. This happened off and on until I was about fifteen years old. I married young and worked on construction and trapped during the winter for several years. One day I decided I needed a new pack basket. I couldn't afford to buy one so I cut down a small tree and made four baskets from it. People saw them and bought them. I've been making them ever since." (In the years since, his baskets have won numerous awards and are displayed in many collections. He and his wife, Sal, have been familiar figures at major folk festivals and crafts shows in the Northeast, demonstrating their baskets and basket-making techniques.)

Eventually, his skills led Smith to quit construction and begin working for himself, making baskets and snow shoes and guiding. "I put an ad up at each of the four local colleges, saying that I would guide students and professors into the hills and mountains for canoeing, hunting, fishing, or hiking. Much to my surprise, I got many interested people. Knowing the animal signs, tracks, trees, fish and birds, I soon found myself giving

101

lectures at colleges on baskets, trapping, hunting and storytelling."

During this same period, Bill Smith also worked at the Higley Flow State Park as a ranger, recreational director, and on the Nature Trail. His guiding for the colleges led to his becoming as an Outdoor Education Teacher for eight years, working first at Canton and then in Parishville with high school students. Meanwhile, he and his wife Sal continued making baskets, with their four children helping them when they could.

In the fall of 1983, Ham Ferry of Sevey's Corners, a well-known Adirondack storyteller, and Smith received a grant from the New York State Council on the Arts through the St. Lawrence Historical Association. The grant enabled Smith to be Ham's "apprentice" for all of that winter, learning Ham's extensive store of old hunting, fishing, and lumbering stories and old poems memorized years ago.

UNCLE CHARLEY'S HUNTIN' TRIP

We lived way back up there in The Featherbed, y'know, and there was a lot of characters lived up in the woods, different old hermits and different people that lived back up in the woods. One of these fellas was named Uncle Charley. At least that's what we called him, anyway. And Charley lived way back in there in a log cabin and it was a nice little cabin. And out in front he had a pond there that used to be a brook but the beavers had dammed it up and made it into a beautiful spring pond. And out behind there there was a couple a acres of land that he kept mowed by hand with a scythe all the time and in the middle of that meadow there was a little garden. Charley always had a nice garden there every year and he would raise all kinds of vegetables. He would have potatoes and corn and cabbages and all that stuff.

This one particular year nothin' seemed to grow right because it rained pretty near all summer long and Charley's vegetables just didn't amount to anything. He went to get his corn and the little ears on the corn wasn't hardly any bigger than your thumb. He went to get his squash and his pumpkins and the

mice had gone right in one side and out the other, ruined all that. Then he decided he would dig his potatoes and there wasn't any of them bigger'n a hen's egg. And he was really discouraged and disgusted and didn't know what he was goin' to do for food for the winter.

So he was sittin' there in his cabin one night thinkin' over the whole business and he's rockin' back and forth and the lamp's lit there on the wall and as he's rockin' he noticed on the other wall this old muzzle-loadin' gun he'd had when he was a kid hung there on a couple pegs. It'd been there for about forty years and of course Charley didn't hunt much anymore so the gun just hung there. And he was thinkin, "I wonder if that old gun would still shoot? If it would, I'd take it down and fix it up and take it out and maybe I could get a deer or something? Or a bear or whatever. I'd get anything I could get."

And so he takes the gun down and he checks the lock all out on it and looks it all over and it looks like it would work all right. And he run a ramrod down the barrel there and it seemed to be all right. So he went into his drawers in his bedroom and he threw all of his clothes out of there and way back in the corner he found some black powder and some lead balls and some stuff there. He brings that out and he put some black powder down that barrel and he ripped a little chunk off his shirttail and wrapped that lead ball in it and he spit on that

105

a couple times and he stuck in that barrel and he rammed it down there with a ramrod. And he got that gun all ready to shoot. And he put it there in the corner and he says, "There, in the mornin' I'll get up bright and early and I'll see if I can't get somethin' t' eat."

Bright and early in the mornin' he got up. He took his old gun and his sandwiches and he went off up through towards Grass River and all the way up that upper tote road and he snuck along there and took his time, still-hunted a little bit. Then he'd sit down there and wait and he sat by one of the best deer trails up there and he still didn't see anything. And he was gettin' more discouraged than ever now and he went up along towards Grass River and he stopped there at noon time and had his lunch. Then he went along down the river and up back down across into the lower tote road and just about dusk he come out through that lower tote road and out into that little meadow, right in back of the camp.

The haze was jes' lifting off that meadow and there was just light enough left so you could see clear over to where the cabin was. And over there, on the right hand side, he thought he caught the glimpse of somethin' movin' over by the big rock ledge. And just as he looked out through there this big doe raised her head up! And boy, he saw her and he got that gun up and he thought "Boy, if I could get that big doe that would give me some meat for winter." So he cocked that gun back and he's all ready to shoot that big doe and all of a sudden on the other side of that rock ledge he thought he saw somethin' else movin'. Then this great big buck raised his head up! He had great big horns, he put his head back down to feed again.

Charley thought, "Boy, if I could get both of those deer that would really gimme some meat for the winter."

Now Charley knew that he only had one shot in that gun, but he was a real fast thinker. And he noticed that on that rock ledge there was a real sharp spot that come down there. And he thought, "If I can hit the edge of that sharp spot I'll split that bullet and kill both of these deer!"

So Old Charley he puts that gun up and he aims at the edge of that rock and he realizes that he's gotta get over there about twenty feet in order to hit it there on the angle that he's gotta hit it and split that bullet and kill both of those deer. He looks over there and he sees that pond about ten foot away and he realizes that the least he's gonna get out of this is wet feet. And Charley's got on a pair of black rubber boots that come up just below his knees with red bands around the top. He's got a pair a big bib overalls on with big pockets in there and hooked up on top there. He's got an overall jacket went over the top of them bib overalls and it used to button right here in the front, but then his belly got in the way so it couldn't hook anymore and it kinda just flopped back and forth in the breeze. And he had an old railroad cap on there that he used to have when he was a young man and he worked on the railroad and it was pretty old and the cardboard had been stickin' out for about five years now in that beak and the bottom part of that where the cloth used to go around was just hangin down kinda like lookin' through lace curtains.

Now Charley eased out there and he's got that gun and he's aimin' at the edge of that rock and he's getting over. And when the deer picked their head up he's got to stop no matter what position he's in. And pretty soon water starts comin' into that right hand boot and pretty soon it's comin' into the left hand boot. And there's water up to his knees and then there's water up to his belt and of course the higher that water gets, the colder it gets. And by the time that water's up here to his chest he's right exactly where he has to be and he aims at the edge of that rock and he cocks that gun back and he looks real careful through there and he touched that thing off! The smoke belched out a that thing and it bellered jes like an old bull! Right through the smoke and fog and everything he could see both of those deer fall right over. That gun hadn't been shot in so long it kicked so hard it knocked him right back into that pond. And he lost his gun and he lost his breath. And he come up out of that pond and he had a beaver in his right hand and a muskrat in his left hand and his pockets was so full a trout that a button popped off his fly and went forty yards through the air and killed a partridge. And he got his whole winter's meat right there in one shot. And that's the story of Uncle Charley's huntin' trip.

"Uncle Charlie's Huntin' Trip" is a brilliantly localized variant of the most widespread of all the Munchhausen tales: "the marvelous hunt." The genius in Smith's telling is in the outrageous contrast between the realistic details in the body of the story and the final explosion into the crescendo of crazy impossibilities. Bill Smith's skill in the control of the pace of the narrative is the mark of a master yarnspinner.

SELECTED BIBLIOGRAPHY

Primary Source

Allen, Ethan. *A Narrative of Col. Ethan's Captivity*. Walpole, N.H.: Thomas and Thomas, 1807.

Audubon. John James. *Ornithological Biography, Vol. I*. Philadelphia: Judah Dobson, 1831.

Austin, William. *A Book of New England Legends by Samuel Adams Drake*. Boston: Roberts Brothers, 1884.

Barnard, John. *Ashton's Memorial: or an authentick account of the strange adventures and signal deliverance of Mr. Phillip Ashton*. London: Richard Ford and Samuel Chandler, 1726.

Burke, T. A. *"Polly Peablossom's Wedding" and Other Tales*. Philadelphia: T. B. Peters and Brothers, 1851.

Byrd, William. *William Byrd's Histories of the Dividing Line Betwixt Virginia and North Carolina*. William K. Boyd, ed. New York: Dover, 1967.

Carver, Jonathan. *Captain Jonathan Carver's narrative of his capture and subsequent escape from the Indians at the bloody massacre committed by them when Fort William Henry fell into the hands of the French in the year 1757, written by himself*. Reprinted by S. G. Drake. Tragedies of the Wilderness. Boston, 1846.

Crockett, David. *A Narrative of the Life of David Crockett of the State of Tennessee*, 1843. Reprint Knoxville: University of Tennessee Press, 1973.

Franklin, Benjamin. *Benjamin Franklin's Letters to the Press, 1758–1775*. Ed. Verner W. Crane. Chapel Hill: University of North Carolina Press, 1950.

Flint, Timothy. *Recollections of the Last Ten Years*. Boston: Cummings, Hillard & CO., 1826.

111

Johnson, Captain Edward. *Wonderworking Providence of Sion's Savior in New England.* London, 1654. Reprint. J. F. Jameson. New York: Scribner's Sons, 1910.

Raspe, RE, *et al. Singular Travels, Campaigns, and Adventures of Baron Munchausen.* New York: Dover reprint, 1960.

Shepherd, Esther. *Paul Bunyan.* New York: Harcourt, Brace, 1924.

Secondary Sources

Aswell, James R., *et al. God Bless the Devil! Liars' Bench Tales,*! Reprint. Knoxville: University of Tennessee Press, 1985.

Bethke, Robert. *Adirondack Voices: Woodsmen and Woodslore.* Chicago: University of Chicago Press, 1981.

Blair, Walter. *Tall Tale America.* New York: Coward-McCann. 1944.

Brunvand, Jan Harold. "Len Henry: North Idaho Munchausen." *Northwest Folklore 1.* (1965), 11–19.

Crane, Charles, Edward. *Winter in Vermont.* New York: Alfred A. Knopf, 1941.

Clough, Ben, ed. *The American Imagination at Work: Tall Tales and Folk Tales.* New York: Alfred A. Knopf, 1947.

Cutting, Edith E. *Lore of an Adirondack County.* Ithaca, N.Y.: Cornell University Press, 1944.

Davidson, Sergeant Bull. *Tall Tales They Tell in the Services.* New York: Thomas Y. Crowell Co., 1943.

Dorson, Richard M. *Bloodstoppers and Bearwalkers.* Cambridge, Mass.: Harvard University Press, 1952.

_____. *Jonathan Draws the Long Bow,*" Cambridge, Mass.: Harvard University Press, 1946.

_____. "The Johnny-Cake Papers." *Journal of American Folklore.* 58. (1945).

Fowke, Edith. "In Defense of Paul Bunyan." *New York Folklore 5.* (1979), 43–51.

Gardner, Emelyn Elizabeth. *Folklore from the Schoharie*

Hills, New York. Ann Arbor: University of Michigan Press, 1937.

Gould, John. *Farmer Takes a Wife*. New York: William Morrow & Company, 1945.

Hazard, Thomas Robinson. *The Johnny Cake Papers of "Shepherd Town"* Boston: The Merrymount Press. Printed for the subscribers, 1915.

Irving, Pierre M. *Life and Letters of Washington Irving*. New York: G. P. Putnam and Son, 1867.

Lunt, Richard K. "Jones Tracy: Tall-Tale Hero from Mount Desert Island." *Northeast Folklore Quarterly 10*, 1968, 1–75.

Lee, Hector. *Folklore of the Mormon Country: J. Golden Kimball Stories, Together with the Brother Petersen Yarns*. Sharon, Conn.: Folk Legacy Records, Inc., FTA-25, 1964.

Stockton, Frank R. *A Storyteller's Pack*. New York: Charles Scribner's Sons, 1897.

Studer, Norman. "Yarns of a Catskill Woodsman." *New York Folklore Quarterly* (1955), 183–92.

Thompson, Harold W. *Body, Boots, and Britches: Folktales, Ballads, and Speech from Country New York*, 1939. Reprint New York: Dover, 1967.

Welsch, Roger. *Catfish at the Pump: Humor and the Frontier*. Lincoln, Neb.: Plains Heritage, 1982.

———. *Shingling the Fog and Other Plains Lies*. Chicago: Swallow Press, 1972.

Folklore Analysis, Oral Tradition, and Comic Theory

Aarne, Antii. *The Types of the Folktale: A Classification and Bibliography*. Translated by Stith Thompaon. New York: Burt Franklin, 1971.

Allen, Barbara, and Lynwood Montell. "Submerged Forms of Historical Truth." *Memory to History: Using Oral Sources in Local Historical Research*. Nashville: American Association for State and Local History, 1981.

Abrahams, Roger D. "Folklore and Literature as Performance." *Journal of the Lore Institute 9*, 1972, 75–94.

Baughman, Ernest W. *Type and Motif Index of the Folk-tales of New England and North America*. The Hague: Mouton and Company, 1966.

Blair, Walter. *Horse Sense in American Humor from Benjamin Franklin to Ogden Nash*. Chicago: University of Chicago Press, 1942.

_____. *Native American Humor*. New York: American Book Company, 1937.

_____, and Hamlin Hill. *American Humor*. New York: Oxford Press, 1978.

Bauman, Richard. "Verbal Art as Performance." *Journal of American Folklore* 77. June 1975, 290–311.

_____. "Differential Identity and the Social Base of Folklore." *Journal of American Folklore 84*, January/March 1971, 31–41.

Biebuyck-Gutz, Brunhilde. "This is the Dyin' Truth: Mechanics of Lying." *Journal of the Folklore Institute 14*, 1977, 73–95.

Beaver, J. Russell. "From Reality to Fantasy: Opening-Closing Formulas in the Structures of American Tall Tales." *Southern Folklore Quarterly 36*. 1972, 369–82.

Boatright, Mody. *Folk Laughter on the American Frontier*. New York: MacMillan, 1949; Collier Books, 1961.

Brown, Carolyn S. *The Tall Tale in American Folklore and Literature*. Knoxville: University of Tennessee Press, 1987.

Corrigan, Robert W. "Comedy and the Comic Spirit." *Comedy: Meaning and Form*. Scranton, Pa.: Chandler Publishing Co., 1965, 18–60.

Cothran, Kay. "Talking Trash in the Okefenoke Swamp Rim, Georgia." *Journal of American Folklore 87*, 1974, 340–356.

Davis, Gerald L. *I Got the Word in Me and I Can Sing It, You Know*. Philadelphia: University of Pennsylvania, 1985.

Dondore, Dorothy. "Big Talk! The Flyting, the Bage, and the Frontier Boast." *American Speech 6*, 1930, 45–55.

Dorson, Richard M. *Folklore and Fakelore: Essays Toward*

a Discipline of Folk Studies. Cambridge, Mass.: Harvard University Press, 1976.

_____. *Man and Beast in Comic Legend*. Bloomington, Ind.: Indiana University Press, 1982.

Dundes, Alan. "Texture, Text, and Context." *Southern Folklore Quarterly 28*, 1964, 251–265.

Freud, Sigmund. "Jokes and the Comic." *Comedy: Meaning and Form*. Robert W. Corrigan, ed. Scranton, Pa.: Chandler, 1965.

Frye, Northrup. *Anatomy of Criticism: Four Essays*. Princeton, N.J.: Princeton University Press, 1957.

Georges, Robert. "Towards an Understanding of Storytelling Events." *Journal of American Folklore 57*, 1944, 97–106.

Gurewitch, Morton L. *Comedy: The Irrational Vision*. Ithaca: Cornell University Press, 1975.

Harpham, Geoffrey Galt. *On the Grotesque: Strategies of Contradiction in Art and Literature*. Princeton, N.J.: Princeton University Press, 1982.

Hymes, Dell. "Models of the Interaction of Language and Social Life." *Directions in Sociolinguistics*. New York: Holt, Rinehart, and Winstron, 1972.

Kenney, W. Howland. *Laughter in the Wilderness: Early American Humor to 1783*. Kent, Ohio: Kent State University Press, 1976.

Labor, William, and Joshua Waletzky. "Narrative Analysis: Oral Versions of Personal Experience." *Essays on the Verbal and Visual Arts*. June Helen, Ed. Seattle: Proceedings of the 1966 Annual Spring Meetings of the American Ethnological Society, 1966.

Lacourciere, Luc. *Oral Tradition: New England and French Canada*. Quebec: Archives de Folklore, Universete" Laval, 1972.

Langer, Suzanne. "The Comic Rhythm." *Feeling and Form*. New York: Charles Scribner's Sons., 1953, 326–350.

Loomis, C. Grant. "The Tall Tale and the Miraculous." *California Folklore Quarterly 4*, 1945, 109–128.

Lord, Alfred B. *The Singer of Tales*. New York: Atheneum, 1971.

Masterson, James R. "Travelers' Tales of Colonial Natural History." *Journal of American Folklore 59*, 1946, 174–188.

Roberts, Warren. "The Art of Perpendicular Lying." *Journal of the Folklore Institute 2*, 1965, 180–219.

Rosenberg, Bruce A. *The Art of the American Folk Preacher*. New York: Oxford University Press, 1970.

Rourke, Constance. *American Humor: A Study of the National Character*, 1931. Reprint New York: Harcourt, Brace, Jovanovich, 1959.

Rubin, Louis D. *The Comic Imagination in American Literature*. New Brunswick, N.J.: Rutgers University Press, 1973.

Ryle, Gilbert. *The Concept of Mind*. New York: Barnes and Noble, 1950.

Sorrell, Walter. *Fools of Comedy*. New York: Grosset and Dunlap, 1972.

Stahl, Sandra K. D. "The Personnel Narrative as Folklore." *Journal of the Folklore Institute, 14*, 1977, 9–30.

Sypher, Wylie. "The Meaning of Comedy." *Comedy: Meaning and Form*. Robert W. Corrigan, ed. Scranton, Pa.: Chandler Publishing Company, 1965, 18–60.

Thompson, Harold W. and Henry Seidel Canby. "Humor." *Literary History of the United States*. Robert Spiller, ed. New York: MacMillan, 1957, 728.

Thompson, Stith. *The Folktale*, 1946. Reprint Berkeley: University of California Press, 1977.

Tolken, Barre. *The Dynamics of Folklore*. Boston: Houghton Mifflin, 1979.

Welsford, Enid. *The Fool: His Social and Literary History*. London: Faber and Faber, 1935.